To Anthony

From
— Grandma & Grandpa
Fox

Sept 28th 2005

OTTO

Goes to Bed

Todd Parr

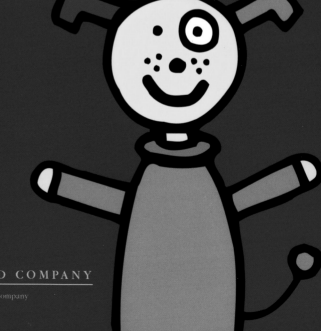

Megan Tingley Books

LITTLE, BROWN AND COMPANY

New York · An AOL Time Warner Company

To Mom
Love, Todd

Also by Todd Parr

The Best Friends Book
Big & Little
Black & White
The Daddy Book
Do's and Don'ts
The Feel Good Book
The Feelings Book
Funny Faces
Going Places
It's Okay to Be Different
The Mommy Book
My Really Cool Baby Book
The Okay Book
Things That Make You Feel Good / Things That Make You Feel Bad
This Is My Hair
Underwear Do's and Don'ts
Zoo Do's and Don'ts

First Edition

Library of Congress Cataloging-in-Publication Data
Parr, Todd.
Otto goes to bed / Todd Parr.—1st ed.
    p. cm.
Summary: Otto the dog doesn't want to go to bed until he
discovers how nice it is to dream.
ISBN 0-316-73873-5
    [1. Dogs—Fiction. 2. Bedtime—Fiction. 3. Dreams—Fiction.] I. Title.
PZ7.P2447 Or 2003
[E]—dc21   2002075436

10 9 8 7 6 5 4 3 2 1

TWP

Printed in Singapore

Otto doesn't want to come inside and go to bed.

He wishes he didn't have to stop doing all the fun things he does all day, like . . .

chasing his tail,

rolling in the mud,

and barking at the cat.

He tries taking a big
bubble bath.

But that doesn't make
him want to go to bed.

He tries brushing his teeth with chicken-flavored toothpaste.

But that doesn't make him want to go to bed.

He tries barking at
the moon.

But that doesn't make
him want to go to bed.

Finally he takes his favorite toy and gets into bed.

He closes his eyes and tries to dream about all the things he wishes he could do, like . . .

jumping on the bed,

eating all the hot dogs
he wants,

and being a superhero!

Then Otto falls fast asleep.
And now he loves going to bed.

SWEET DREAMS, OTTO!

Sometimes it's hard to go to bed, ⭐ but remember, it's more fun when you dream about all your favorite things!

Love, ♡

OTTO and TODD